PEANUTS
Happy
Thanksgiving,
SNOOPY!

By Charles M. Schulz
Adapted by Jason Cooper
Illustrated by Scott Jeralds

SIMON SPOTLIGHT
New York London Toronto Sydney New Delhi

SIMON SPOTLIGHT
An imprint of Simon & Schuster Children's Publishing Division
1230 Avenue of the Americas, New York, New York 10020
This Simon Spotlight paperback edition September 2018
© 2018 Peanuts Worldwide LLC
SIMON SPOTLIGHT and colophon are registered trademarks of Simon & Schuster, Inc.
For information about special discounts for bulk purchases, please contact Simon & Schuster
Special Sales at 1-866-506-1949 or business@simonandschuster.com.
Manufactured in the United States of America 0718 LAK
2 4 6 8 10 9 7 5 3 1
ISBN 978-1-5344-2528-6 (pbk)
ISBN 978-1-5344-2529-3 (eBook)

Charlie Brown loves Thanksgiving. Every year he travels to visit his grandmother and shares a large, wonderful meal with his family. It's a very special tradition.

This year, however, is going to be different . . .

"I just got off the phone with Grandma," Charlie Brown tells his sister, Sally. "She can't host Thanksgiving this year! She'll be out of town."

"What about our other grandma?" Sally asks.

"She's mountain biking in Toronto!" says Charlie Brown.

"Oh, well. At least she's staying active," Sally says.

Lucy and her family have their own Thanksgiving tradition. Usually she and her brothers, Linus and Rerun, help their parents make a pumpkin pie for dessert. But this year Linus doesn't feel like participating.

"I don't think I'll help with the pie this year," Linus says.
Lucy can't believe her ears. "Why not?!" she asks.
"It's difficult to admit," Linus explains, "but I simply don't care for pumpkin pie."
Lucy looks confused.

Rerun also refuses to help. "I don't care for pumpkin pie, either," he says.

Lucy is shocked. "I can't believe this!" she shouts.

"Maybe we can have cold cereal," Rerun suggests.

"You can't have cereal at Thanksgiving!" Lucy says.

"But cereal is delicious!" Rerun tells her. "And sometimes there's a prize in the box!"

Peppermint Patty has to change her Thanksgiving plans this year, too. Her father works a lot, but he always has Thanksgiving off so they can spend it together—but this year he has to go on a business trip during the holiday.

Peppermint Patty has an idea. She calls her friend Marcie. "Say, Marcie, how would you like to spend Thanksgiving with me?" she asks.

"I'm sorry, sir. I'm so sick, all I can do is sleep and eat soda crackers," Marcie whispers weakly.

"But it's Thanksgiving! What am I supposed to do?" Peppermint Patty asks.

"Just do what I'm going to do," Marcie says. "Stay in bed and be thankful for soda crackers."

This is shaping up to be an unusual Thanksgiving for everyone—everyone except Snoopy. He is spending this holiday the way he always does. By wearing sunglasses, leaning on his doghouse, and pretending his name is Joe Cool.

Snoopy has an active imagination. Here's Joe Cool standing outside his dorm. He's got the whole campus to himself! Snoopy thinks. Everyone has split for Thanksgiving Break. No classes! No worries!

But Joe Cool doesn't always feel quite as "cool" as he's pretending to be. *No friends and no fun, either,* Snoopy sighs. *No one ever invites Joe Cool home for Thanksgiving,* he thinks.

Meanwhile, to help clear his mind, Charlie Brown decides to take a walk. He winds up at his school playground. He sees his friends Peppermint Patty and Lucy sitting on the swings.

"Happy Thanksgiving, Chuck!" Peppermint Patty says.

"Things are not going to be the same this year." Charlie Brown sighs.

"I can't believe my lousy brothers ruined Thanksgiving!" Lucy complains.

"At least your family is here and not selling insurance in Petaluma," Peppermint Patty says.
They all feel sorry for themselves.

Then they see Joe Cool, looking sad too.

Here's Joe Cool, Snoopy thinks, *walking over the river, through the woods . . . aimlessly across the vacant college campus.* Then he looks at Charlie Brown and sighs.

"You know," Peppermint Patty says, "I think Snoopy may be sad, too."

"Why? He doesn't celebrate Thanksgiving!" Lucy says.

"Maybe he wants to!" Peppermint Patty declares. "Charlie Brown, do you do anything nice for your dog on Thanksgiving?"

Charlie Brown blushes. "Well, I bring him supper before we leave for Grandma's house."

"A *nice* supper?" Lucy asks.

"No, just his normal food," Charlie Brown admits.

"Thanksgiving is a time to celebrate with friends and family," Lucy scolds. "Don't you think it makes Snoopy feel left out watching you celebrate every year without him?"

Charlie Brown agrees. He had never thought of that.

"I have an idea!" Charlie Brown proclaims. "Since none of us are having our traditional Thanksgiving this year, let's start a new tradition and celebrate together! And this time, we'll be sure to invite Joe Cool!"

Snoopy hears the idea and smiles. *What's this? An invitation for Joe Cool?* Snoopy pats Charlie Brown on the back, and then jokes, *I'll check my schedule!*

Peppermint Patty likes the idea, too. "Nice thinking, Chuck! But how can we celebrate Thanksgiving with no food? Where's the turkey? Where's the cornbread stuffing? Where are the cranberries shaped like a tin can?"

Snoopy has an idea and rushes off.

I'll handle the food! Snoopy thinks. *Joe Cool always sends out for pizza!*

Snoopy quickly returns, followed by his friend Woodstock, who is smiling and carrying a large square box. Snoopy hands out sunglasses and everyone digs in.

"You know, it's not the Thanksgiving we expected," Charlie Brown says, "but it's one we'll never forget!"